Chandrabhushan

Ayush Kumar Singh

Chandrabhushan

This edition is the English translation of the original Hindi work titled, चन्द्रभूषण।

Declaration

This book is a work of fiction. All characters, places, events, and dialogues described in this book are the result of the author's imagination. Any resemblance to any living or deceased person, community, institution, or place is purely coincidental. The author's intention is not to hurt the sentiments of any individual or group.

Ayush Kumar Singh

22/11/2025

New Delhi

Chandrabhushan

Synopsis

This novel is the story of extraordinary struggles in an ordinary village, centered on the youngest son of the family, Chandrabhushan. Amidst family divisions, greed, the weight of traditions, and crumbling relationships, he grows up as the only child who holds on to truth, honour, and love. After losing his mother in childhood, he witnesses his father's struggles, his brother's quarrels, and the harsh customs of society with his own eyes. Through study and hard work, he forges his own path, but life also leads him down the difficult road of love, defiance, and justice. Marriage to a minor, court rulings, and the narrow-mindedness of the village, through all this, he learns the true meaning of responsibility and courage.

Chandrabhushan's journey shows that no matter how deep poverty, division, and injustice run, truth and

Chandrabhushan

human values are what make a person "the moon of the family and the pride of society."

Author: Ayush Kumar Singh

1: Dhanwar Pur

In the small village of Dhanwar Pur in Bihar's Saharsa district, the morning air always carried the scent of earth, sunlight, and fresh hope. It was a fragrance that, despite the daily struggles, made you feel the continuity of life. In the unpaved lanes, cows and buffaloes ambled at their own leisurely pace, the tinkling of their neck bells forming the village's dawn music. Women bent over the well to draw water; the chime of their bangles and their soft chatter filled the air. And from every home rose the faint smell of wood-smoke from the hearth, announcing that the day had begun and another journey through hardship had started.

In the heart of this village, under the shade of a large banyan tree, stood the house of Ramlakhan Thakur. It was old but sturdy, as if it were telling the story of the family's history. Its thick walls held the joys and sorrows of many generations. These days, the house was a little busier than usual, because the wedding of the middle son, Mohan, had been fixed. This bustle wasn't just about noise. It showed in the faint tension on every face, in the hidden excitement and unspoken worries.

As Janki Devi sprinkled water in the courtyard, she called out, "Rukmani! Get the saree that was set aside for the bride, Mohan's in-laws are sending people over."

Rukmani hurriedly opened the cupboard. "I'll get it now, Maayi."

On the veranda, Ramlakhan Thakur took a drag from his hookah and said, "The expenses for Mohan's wedding are rising too much. How will this be managed all alone?"

The eldest daughter-in-law, Sunaina, with the end of her dupatta draped over her head, spoke up, "Babu ji, when we were married, you managed everything. You'll manage for Mohan too." There was a hint of pride in her voice.

Mohan stepped out and said, "Bhabhi, don't worry about me. I'll cover half the expenses myself."

Sunaina smiled. "Oh, you fool! Who's ever heard of the groom paying for his own wedding? It's all the family's responsibility."

It was afternoon. In different corners of the house, each person's world was both shrinking and expanding in its own way.

Rukmani sat in a quiet nook of the courtyard, an old sewing machine making its tick-tick sound in front of her. She had learned sewing at a nearby training centre and was now practising. Her fingers carefully guided the fabric under the needle. This work not only offered her a path toward self-reliance but also served as a safe refuge. Sitting here, she could escape her sister-in-law's sharp remarks and the anxieties surrounding marriage. She was skillfully mending a torn portion of a small cotton saree.

On the other side, inside the room, Mohan sat with books spread open on a small table. Notes for competitive exams lay scattered before him. Amidst the wedding preparations, he had kept up with his studies. He knew that after marriage his responsibilities would only increase, and farming alone wouldn't allow him to give his future family all that he hoped for. There was a quiet determination in his eyes. Sometimes he would lose himself in his books; other times the thought of the wedding would fill him with restlessness. Studying was his escape, it lifted him out of the entanglements of the present and carried him toward the possibilities of the future.

After all, for those who have nothing, study remains the only way, both to navigate difficulties and to build a future. In today's new era, some may consider government employment old-fashioned, but the truth is that for those without access to expensive colleges, costly courses, or strong family backing, such a job becomes a reliable anchor.

Studying itself requires money, and when your pockets are empty, you're left with only one thing: hard work.

And that hard work must be pursued with honest intent, not with tears streaming down your face, but with clarity of purpose.

In a corner of the courtyard, Chandrabhushan sat shaping a boat out of clay. His small fingers were giving form to the mud. His world was the clearest and most innocent. His boat wasn't just made of clay, it was a vessel for his imagination, one that could take him beyond the walls of this house to some unknown, faraway land. Once he finished the boat, he would float it in a bowl of water and beam with joy.

Mohan called out to him, "Chandru! Come, we need to get the kurta I'll wear for the wedding."

Chandrabhushan looked up. "Bhai, will we get to dance in the wedding procession too?"

Mohan laughed. "You'll be dancing right at the front, you! You'll ride on the horse with the groom."

Chandru's eyes sparkled. Perhaps there was no greater happiness in the world for him.

Amidst the wedding preparations, Rukmani worked quietly. Sunaina, the eldest sister-in-law, made a jibe: "Rukmani, your age is passing by. Father-in-law should start thinking about you too."

Rukmani flushed red with embarrassment but said nothing. She pressed the sewing machine pedal harder, as if the noise of her machine alone could drown out her sister-in-law's words.

Savitri Devi gently scolded, "Sunaina, not everything is to be said as a joke."

Sunaina pursed her lips and went inside.

Rukmani noticed that Mohan had also heard this exchange, and there was a strange helplessness on his face. She continued with her sewing. She thought, If only my life were like this piece of cloth, I could use my skill to mend its torn parts. But the fragments of her own life, it seemed, lay in the hands of others.

Amidst the wedding's joy, there was also a quiet tension: sometimes Sunaina's sharp remarks, sometimes worries about the expenses, sometimes the villagers' talk. Outside, sitting at the village square, the elders remarked, "Once Mohan's wedding is over, you'll see a new turn in Thakur's household.

Chandrabhushan silently watched everything.

Sometimes he saw his mother's exhaustion, sometimes his father's worry, sometimes his sister-in-law's sharp tone, sometimes Rukmani's silence. He observed how Rukmani didi would lose herself in her sewing, how Mohan bhaiya would immerse himself in his books, while he himself kept making his clay boat.

Even at his young age, he had understood that happiness in this house was not as simple as it appeared from the outside. Everyone, in their own world, was wrestling with some kind of struggle.

He did not know then that this wedding, this house, and this village would, in time, become the true beginning of his life. The clay boat he was making today would one day set him afloat on the deep ocean of life.

2: The Middle Daughter-in-law

The morning's redness had not yet spread completely when the wedding flowers scattered in Ramlakhan Thakur's courtyard wilted and clung to the ground. The pink and red chrysanthemums that had filled the air with fragrance only yesterday now lay crushed, withered, pressed into the earth, as if, along with the wedding's splendour, its freshness too had bid farewell overnight. After the rituals that had gone on through the night, there was activity in the house, but a strange heaviness hung in the air. A weight made of new responsibilities, new hopes, and old fears.

The new bride, Saraswati, was crossing the threshold for the first time. Her new red odhni and yellow saree still carried the scent of the wedding, but an unfamiliar fear was clear in her eyes. She quietly touched the feet of all the elders gathered in the courtyard, and with each obeisance her heart beat with a strange unease.

Rukmani whispered in her ear, "Bhabhi, step carefully. In our house, they expect more from daughters-in-law than they do from their own daughters. You have to think before every step here."

Saraswati tried to smile, but exhaustion and a faint nervousness were plain on her face. She glanced at Rukmani as if wanting to say something but unable to find the words. Rukmani understood her silent question: Will I be able to be happy here?

In the kitchen, Badi Kaki, who was actually Ramlakhan Thakur's sister and the unspoken rule-maker of the household, said in a sharp tone, "O, Saraswati! Go fetch water, and make sure you don't fill it from that earthen pot near the lower leaves. We don't drink that water!"

Saraswati was startled. She couldn't understand how water could have distinctions. Hesitantly, she asked, "Whose water, Kaki?"

"The one from the well near that Chamar's house, down in the basti. You're a daughter-in-law now, don't go asking about boundaries. Just do as you're told."

Saraswati fell silent. In her quietness, the sound of hurt was clearly audible. She went to fetch the water, but many questions churned in her mind. Does water also flow according to caste? Do pots also learn untouchability?

Chandrabhushan was getting ready for school. Slinging his bag over his shoulder, he said to his mother, Savitri Devi, "Maa, the teacher was saying yesterday that I could get a scholarship next year. I just need to study a little more."

His mother lovingly stroked his hair. "Son, you are our light. But after school, grind a little wheat, don't let the new bahu carry too much burden. She's just arrived; we can't put too much on her."

Chandrabhushan smiled, but inside he felt a crack. He knew that the shadows of manual labour and the caste system gnawed at his dreams every day. At school he heard his teachers speak of equality and justice, but at home he was met with discrimination and old rigid customs.

In the afternoon, all the women of the house were sitting on a raised wooden cot in the courtyard. Saraswati was busy near the hearth, learning the ways of her new home, and Sunaina was her teacher. Just then a Dom woman from the neighbourhood, Dhania, appeared at the door.

"Choti bahu, you had called me? Shall I give you the firewood?"

There was a humility in Dhania's voice that had been born from centuries of oppression and humiliation. She stood outside the door, not daring to step inside.

Badi Kaki snapped, "Stay at the door! Don't come inside! Your feet will pollute our courtyard!"

Dhania stopped, shrinking back as if she had expected this reaction all along. There was no surprise on her face, only a deep, resigned quiet.

Saraswati's heart twisted. She felt the ground shift beneath her feet. Gathering courage, she said, "Kaki, firewood burns the same in everyone's hands, doesn't it? Dhania didi was just..."

Kaki's face turned red. "So clever, are you? Come into this house and start preaching justice right away? What do you know of our family's dignity! Do what you're told, nothing more!"

Dhania silently turned away, her eyes lowered. Saraswati's eyes welled up, but she held back the tears. Now she understood why Rukmani had said, "Step carefully."

On his way back from school, Chandrabhushan saw children from the lower basti playing barefoot. Their clothes were torn, but their eyes held the same innocence that he and his friends had. Yet the high-caste children of the village wouldn't even play with them; they would change their path just by looking at them, as if they were a contagious disease.

He asked his friend Ramu, "Why does this happen? Aren't we all the same? Everyone's blood is red, everyone's tears are alike."

Ramu said, "Just leave it, man. That's how it is here. Don't take it to heart. When you grow up, you'll understand."

But something broke inside Chandrabhushan. He felt as though the whole village was living in the stench of an old wound, and everyone had grown used to it. He thought: When I grow up, will I too have to accept all this?

In the evening, an argument broke out in the house. Kaki was yelling at Saraswati: "Bahu, the way you spoke to that low-caste woman today is against our family's traditions! You have to understand, you are now the daughter-in-law of a Thakur household."

Saraswati said tearfully, "Kaki, what wrong did I do? I spoke to a human being as a human being! Dhania didi had simply come to give us firewood."

Sunaina said softly, "Younger one, it's not about humanity here, it's about tradition. Just go along with it; everything will be fine."

Saraswati fell silent, but a rebellion was growing in her silence. She knew that today she had not fought just over firewood, but over her very existence.

Chandrabhushan heard all this; it felt as though a burning ember had dropped into his heart. He saw how his new bhabhi, who only yesterday had shone in the wedding's splendour, was being broken today in the name of tradition.

At night, Chandrabhushan lay on the roof. The stars in the sky were calm, but a storm was rising within him. Everything he had seen today, his sister-in-law's humiliation, Dhania's helplessness, the distance between the village children, swirled in his mind.

He said to himself: I will change something. If I can't change it, then at least I will write and keep showing the truth. The ways of the village traditions, their pain, everything. I will write about how water learns caste, how even firewood comes to know high and low.

This decision was going to change his life. At seven years old, this child had made a vow that, in time, would change not only his own life but the life of the entire village. That night, Chandrabhushan did not merely gaze at the stars, he saw the path of his future.

3: Division

Three months had passed since the wedding. The crowds of relatives were gone now; only the everyday quarrels remained. The wedding's brightness that had filled the house until yesterday had slowly turned into bitterness. Early in the morning, as soon as the rooster crowed, the sharp voices of the two daughters-in-law echoed in the courtyard.

"Sunaina bhabhi, will your daily tantrums ever improve?" Saraswati said in a tired voice. She sat near the hearth making Bread, lines of sweat and worry clear on her forehead.

Sunaina, who as the eldest daughter-in-law considered herself to have special rights, placed a hand on her stomach and retorted, "It's you who needs to improve, you came later, but you act as if you know everything! I'm pregnant. And I can't stand doing your work for you!"

Saraswati couldn't stay quiet. "Being pregnant doesn't mean you get to make new rules for the house! Everyone's health isn't the same, bhabhi."

Their voices grew so loud that Savitri Devi came out of the kitchen. Her face showed deep exhaustion and helplessness. She knew this fight wasn't just about today, it was the result of the bitterness that had been building over the last three months.

Sunaina also yelled at her husband, Shambhunath, every day. Shambhunath was a quiet-natured man, but his wife's constant complaints had worn him down. That night, the same thing happened again.

"Your mother and that younger bahu just won't tolerate me! How am I supposed to live here? Why don't you say something!" Sunaina shrieked. Her voice carried a kind of restlessness and anger that grew worse every day.

Shambhunath, exhausted, could only say, "Sunaina, calm down, for our child's sake, at least."

Sunaina cut him off. "Me, calm? Because of your mother, I end up being the one in the wrong? Just get us a separate house! I want my own hearth now!"

Her voice was so bitter and sharp that it could be heard in the neighbouring houses. The women next door listened from behind their doors, and the next day the whole village would certainly be gossiping about it.

That night, Savitri Devi said to Ramlakhan, her voice carrying a mother's pain and a homemaker's helplessness. "All our lives, in our efforts to educate Mohan, we delayed Rukmani's marriage and now that same Mohan's family is breaking our home apart. When we brought her in as a daughter-in-law, we thought she would brighten the house. But now she's torn it apart with her quarrels."

Ramlakhan took a deep breath. His eyes showed a father's worry and the pain of a family breaking. "Who can explain to Sunaina? She's about to have a child, so she's under more stress. But a home is a home. Once it breaks, it takes years to mend."

Both of them knew that a family's division wasn't just the splitting of hearths, it was the splitting of relationships.

The next morning, Sunaina threw her things around in the kitchen and announced, her face set with stubborn resolve. "That's it! From today, I'm lighting my own separate hearth. Maa ji, you all manage your own affairs now."

Saraswati was stunned. She couldn't believe anyone would break a family like this. "What are you doing? It won't be house against house, it'll be heart against heart!"

Sunaina screamed, "Stay out of this, younger one! My husband will be separate, my fields will be separate, and my hearth will be separate."

And so Ramlakhan had to call a meeting of the village council. For him, this was the hardest decision of all.

That day, the courtyard was filled with everyone, elders, panchayat members, family. Hours of arguments, accusations and counter-accusations, crying and shouting. Everyone fought for their own share.

Finally, the decision came, heavy with sorrow: three hearths.

· First, Ramlakhan and Savitri would keep the main part of the house, where the family's roots lay. Chandrabhushan and Rukmani would stay with them.

· Second, Shambhunath and Sunaina: the room on the eastern side and a separate kitchen.

· Third, Mohan and Saraswati: the room on the western side and a separate kitchen.

The greatest fear of a farming family had come true. Houses don't break from mere separation; hearts break. The courtyard where everyone once sat together to eat now seemed to lead in three different directions.

Chandrabhushan handed his plate to Saraswati and asked softly, his voice holding a child's innocence and sadness. "Bhabhi, why are you upset? You always used to give me food."

His eyes filled with tears. He couldn't understand why everything had suddenly changed.

Saraswati turned her face away; tears were in her eyes too. "Child, now the house has become three pieces. Who can be responsible for whom? I won't be able to give you food every day anymore."

Chandrabhushan fell silent. For the first time, he felt that when a home breaks, children are the first to fall. His world, which until yesterday had been whole and safe, now lay scattered in pieces.

At night he lay on the roof. The stars were above, but below the whole world lay broken. Many questions rose in his mind.

He said to himself silently: When the home itself has been torn apart, what foundation will I grow up with? But I will write. I will write everything truthfully. Surely someone will listen.

He took out a diary and began to write: Today our home broke apart. I've heard that something new is built only after breaking, but what broke today will perhaps never be mended.

The next day, Savitri Devi gently said to Ramlakhan, her voice full of a mother's concern. "We should get Rukmani married. If the girl stays in this house, the taunts and scoldings will only increase. Her life will be ruined."

Ramlakhan bowed his head in sorrow. He was beginning to regret every decision he had made. "I educated Mohan, and in doing so I pushed Rukmani aside. Now I feel I have lost two children at once."

And here the story turns a new corner. Where Rukmani's marriage becomes a necessity, Chandrabhushan's diary becomes his true companion, and the fractured family sets out in search of new relationships. The house where once one hearth burned now held three separate paths, each giving birth to its own stories.

4: Farewell

Ramlakhan had arranged Rukmani's marriage to Abhijit Singh, the son of his distant friend Vinod Singh, as best he could. Now the day of Rukmani's wedding had drawn near, but there was no excitement in the house, only a muffled weight pressing on everyone's chest. In the same house where preparations for Mohan's wedding had once been filled with laughter and teasing, Rukmani's wedding preparations now went on with an unwelcome sense of compulsion.

Ramlakhan sat gazing silently toward the village square, as if searching for an answer from the elders gathered there. His eyes held a father's pain, the pain that, even on the joyous occasion of sending off a daughter, was suffocating under the pressure of society.

Savitri Devi was steeped in constant worry. "Is our daughter's fate also written the same as that of other girls in the village? Without two-and-a-half to three lakh rupees, no one will even talk." In her hands she held Rukmani's wedding saree, but her eyes carried questions far heavier than that saree.

Meanwhile, Abhijit, the only son of his family, was lost in anxious thought. "What should I do? On one side, Uncle Ramlakhan's helplessness; on top of that, how will this wedding even happen? Let me do one thing, I'll arrange some of the tilak items myself. At least his honour will be saved; no one else will know."

He took out the money he had saved from his own pocket, a small amount accumulated over months of hard work. He thought carefully and made the purchases: a set of steel utensils, two brass ones, and some flower decorations. "This is all I could manage, but at least in the eyes of the village, something will be visible." In this small effort of his lay the love of a life-partner. Men with such a pure heart are rarely born. In this world, most people become so fierce in their greed for dowry that they tear at others like wild wolves. But this young man, who let go of the lure of dowry and instead shouldered the honour of his wife's family, was truly exceptional, a bright lamp of civility, sensitivity, and humanity, shining alone in a dark crowd.

As soon as the news of the wedding began to spread through the village like the wind, an endless wave of questions and speculation ran through the entire village. The elders sitting under the peepal tree at the square, the women filling pitchers at the well, the farmers sweating on the edges of the fields, everyone's tongue echoed the same mantra:

"What will she get in dowry?"

"Sending a daughter away completely empty-handed is considered inauspicious."

"It's the custom of society; it has to be followed."

"When has individual feeling ever mattered against tradition?"

People had always heard it said that it was the groom's side that demanded dowry, but here the scene was reversed. The real pressure was being carried by society itself, caste, community, neighbourhood, all of them.

"The bride's family must give something; otherwise, where is the dignity in a wedding?"

Ramlakhan's chest began to feel as if it were being crushed by an invisible weight. Every voice, every taunt, every piece of traditional 'advice' gnawed at him from within. It seemed to him as if the entire village together was loading a mountain of responsibilities onto his back.

The same painful question flashed through his mind again and again: Will my daughter's fate truly be judged by how much dowry she takes to her new home?

From each of the three hearths, rice was being cooked separately. Yet the air carried not the fragrance of celebration, but a silence that screamed the helplessness of every heart.

Saraswati, roasting bread on the hearth, looked at Rukmani. "Dear child, every girl dreams of her wedding. But when the home has already broken, even dreams become incomplete." Her voice carried both a sister-in-law's love and a woman's understanding.

Rukmani simply remained quiet. There was no glow on her face at the thought of marriage, only a frightened acceptance. She too knew: "I'm not a child anymore, but because of the family's circumstances, I'm being sent to my in-laws." She had put her sewing machine aside, as if bidding farewell to her own dreams.

Chandrabhushan sat in a corner, balancing a book on his head as if trying to escape from the world. His eyes held the question: When will our house be whole again?

On the wedding day, turmeric was applied in the courtyard, the dholak was played, neighbours arrived, but their faces showed more sympathy than joy. Everyone knew that this wedding was born not of love but of the compulsion of circumstances.

The eldest daughter-in-law, Sunaina, stood with her son in her arms. Savitri Devi would occasionally hold the child and try to smile, but the water welled up in her eyes and told everything. She knew that today it wasn't only her daughter who was being sent away, her dream was also being completed.

The wedding procession arrived, there was a crowd, and the comments of the village women were clearly audible. "The dowry seems a bit modest. Still, she's getting a good family. Some people don't get that even after giving lakhs."

Ramlakhan's heart felt a surge of relief.

Time had matured Chandrabhushan as well. Today, when he saw Rukmani walking toward the doli, his steps faltered. The tears in Rukmani's eyes seemed to fall directly onto his heart. Those tears that the world might see as merely the soft moisture of ritual, for a brother, they were like a silent wail.

As she approached the doli, Rukmani turned once to look back at her home, her courtyard, her childhood. That single glance pierced Chandrabhushan to his core. In that moment, he understood: a farewell doesn't just tire a sister's feet; it suddenly ages a brother's heart as well.

He gently held his sister's hand, as if wanting to say that bonds that exist for lifetimes do not break by crossing a doli's threshold. But the words did not reach his lips, because there are some sorrows that only a brother can understand, and some acts of composure that only a sister can perform.

5: Flight

Not even a month had passed since Rukmani's farewell when a new wind of fragmentation began to blow through the house. The middle son, Mohan, had become adamant about going to Delhi. He had completed his B.Sc., and there had even been talk of a job in an office in Saharsa's market, but his mind no longer felt settled in this small town.

"I'll find a decent job in Delhi. Here in the village, only farming and quarrels remain," he would tell his father, a strange restlessness in his eyes, like a bird trapped in a cage, gazing at the sky.

Savitri Devi understood in her heart that her son was thinking correctly, yet she was afraid. "City life isn't easy, my son. There, you have no one of your own, no support." Her voice clearly carried a mother's fear.

But Saraswati, the gentle, sensible daughter-in-law with her light smile, said plainly one day: "Father, both of us are going to Delhi. The daily tension here is hollowing Mohan out."

Ramlakhan remained silent. His eyes showed a father's defeat and a farmer's helplessness. The thread of the family was fraying, and he could not hold it together.

When Mohan and Saraswati were about to leave, the villagers tossed their comments around like the wind.

"Look, the eldest son stayed here, now the middle one is running off to the city."

"What work would an educated man find in the village anyway?"

"Once he's in Delhi, he'll send money back; the household will manage."

But in Saraswati's eyes there was only one concern: "What will become of Chandrabhushan? He's the one we all doted on." Secretly, she placed twenty rupees in Chandrabhushan's palm. "Don't stop studying. You'll go very far."

Chandrabhushan said nothing, but his small smile seemed to waver. He touched Saraswati's feet, taking a long, wordless farewell. Many questions stirred in his mind: Will I now be left completely alone? Will there be anyone left to listen to anything about my studies?

With Mohan and Saraswati gone, a great support had vanished. Sunaina had always been quick to anger; now she flared up at the smallest spark, like dry wood. The atmosphere in the house was becoming more and more toxic.

Chandrabhushan's days too wore on. Mornings meant feeding the cows and buffaloes, picking up dung, sweeping the courtyard, drawing water from the well. Doing all this left his palms covered in blisters. He would take ten rupees and walk toward school; by the time he arrived, his feet were white with dust. When he sat in class, the teacher would ask, "Will you study, or just waste your life in the fields?" Chandrabhushan would simply smile quietly. He knew that the family's poverty, the pain of the partition, the strife between brothers all of it loomed larger than his books.

Afternoons: return from school, work in the fields. Evenings: come home, open a book for a few moments, and alongside that, see Ramlakhan sitting silent in pain, and in Savitri's eyes an ocean of worry.

Amidst all this, Chandrabhushan understood one thing more clearly each day: "My education is not my compulsion, it is my liberation."

What glory was there in village education compared to what city schools could offer? Here, learning was not a priority of life; it remained a difficult penance. Childhoods were spent on the edges of fields. Nearly seventy percent of children, as soon as they saw the morning light, went after the plough and bullocks. Twenty percent dropped their books along the way. The weight of hunger, poverty, and responsibilities was heavier than their notebooks filled with pages. And then there remained those ten percent whom neither the sun could stop, nor the rain, nor the wounds of circumstance. Chandrabhushan was one of those rare children who wanted to rise from the earth and make education the lamp of his life. Amid broken benches, incomplete classes, and the help of one or two teachers, he was weaving the cocoon of his dreams, as if even in Bihar's dilapidated education system there was some corner where hope still breathed.

Sunaina would taunt, "Studying, studying all the time, who's going to do the housework? When Mohan was here, he did everything. Now it's all on us!"

Ramlakhan would try to pacify her: "Beti, he's just a child; let him study."

Sunaina would retort, "Who's going to look after my affairs? Am I going to go off to some city?"

But it was Savitri Devi who stood by him every day, bringing both hot bread and courage. "Son, you study. Change the fortune of our house, my son."

Chandrabhushan only nodded, a fire blazing inside him. He knew that his studies were not merely his own; they carried the hopes of the whole family.

Chandrabhushan was not alone. He had two true friends: Ramu and Bittu. Ramu was from the lower basti, but his mind was exceptionally sharp. Bittu's family was also poor, but his dreams were large. The three of them studied together, dreamed together, and lifted each other's spirits.

One day the three sat under an old banyan tree outside the village. Ramu said, "Chandru, you're going to go very far. Your writing is excellent."

Chandrabhushan replied, "But you see how things are at home. Father says they'll take me out of school next year."

Bittu gave him courage: "We won't let that happen. The three of us will give tuitions together. We'll teach younger children and earn money."

Thus began Chandrabhushan's new battle, the battle to continue his education. The three friends started teaching the small children of the village. At first people laughed, but when their children's marks improved, people's attitudes changed.

Chandrabhushan wrote in his diary: Today we took our first tuition class. Ramu, Bittu, and I taught five children together. Perhaps this is the way, to support one another, to give wings to one another's dreams.

He knew now that he was not studying only for himself, but for his family, and for that village from which change could begin. And with that resolve he kept moving forward, one step toward his education, one step toward his dreams.

6: Mahamaya

•

Chandrabhushan had now reached the tenth standard, and his world had shrunk to the three-kilometre footpath that took him from home to school and back again. Feet soaked in the morning dew of the fields, dusty roads at noon, and a return laden with exhaustion in the evening, this had become his daily life. But within this ordinary existence an extraordinary dream was growing, and that dream was his mother, Savitri Devi. She was not merely his mother; she was half his courage. Every morning when he left for school, she would bless him and say, "Son, education never lets a person go hungry. If you study, you will eat your two meals with honour." These words were like a mantra for Chandrabhushan, giving him fresh energy in every weariness and despair. The family's financial condition was not good, but Savitri Devi never let him stop studying. Sometimes she would break apart her small savings to pay his school fees; other times she would go hungry herself yet pack a tiffin for him. At night, even after being utterly spent with exhaustion, she would look at his notebooks and offer suggestions for improvement. The light that shone in her eyes was the greatest inspiration in Chandrabhushan's world.

But slowly, his mother's health began to decline. First a light cough, then tightness in the chest, and then a fatigue that sometimes seemed like fainting. Chandrabhushan often suggested taking her to town to see a proper doctor, but Savitri Devi always put it off. "It's nothing, just the change of seasons." The village doctor merely said, "She is anaemic; keep giving the medicine." But the truth was that Savitri Devi was crumbling from within, not only physically, but mentally as well. The division of the family, the departure of her daughters, and now the changing circumstances of the house had broken her.

The atmosphere in the house grew more toxic by the day. Now only the eldest brother, Shambhunath, his wife Sunaina, and their child, Lav, remained in the house. Sunaina was becoming increasingly irritable and harsh. Bickering in the kitchen, taunts, anger, everything seemed to be vented on her. Sometimes she would say in a voice loud enough to be heard clearly: "All the work falls on me, on top of that my mother-in-law's illness, and this youngest brother just keeps studying, studying! How long will he keep studying? He doesn't earn anything either! Even after the partition, why should I have this headache?" Chandrabhushan heard all this but remained silent. His mother wanted him not to listen, just to keep studying, but he could not run away from his mother's pain. He saw how she would quietly continue her work even after hearing Sunaina's taunts, and at night, when he studied, she would come and sit beside him, as if watching him study made all her sorrows disappear.

Then came that dark night. When Chandrabhushan returned from school, he saw his mother lying on the cot, her breath rapid, the medicine no longer helping. Her face had turned pale and her eyes were sunken. He rushed to her side and took her hand. Savitri Devi, with trembling hand, placed it on his head and said softly, "Son, never stop studying, and never take the wrong path, no matter what the world says. You are our dream." In her eyes was that gleam that only a mother sees in her child's future. But her body was giving way. Chandrabhushan held her hand firmly and said, "Mother, get well. Tomorrow I'll take you to town to a good doctor." But Savitri Devi shook her head with a smile, as if to say it was too late. That night, with her head in the lap of her beloved son, Savitri Devi's breaths ceased.

The next day, flames rose on the funeral pyre at the ghat. The air was heavy, the sky echoing with sobs. Tears trickled from Chandrabhushan's eyes, but he could not cry out; it was as if his voice had choked in his throat. He felt that his world had ended. His mother was his home, and now only walls remained. But that night, as he sat alone in the mud-walled room, he opened his books. His eyes were red, yet the words were clear. He whispered, "Mother, you will see, I will not give up my studies. I will become something." And from this moment began Chandrabhushan's struggle in its truest sense. Now he was studying not only for himself, but to fulfil his mother's dream. Every word, every page, every lesson reminded him of that final promise, which had shown him a new path to live.

After his mother's death, the house no longer felt like a home. The walls were the same, but the warmth of occupancy had gone. Chandrabhushan often thought that a home is built not of bricks and stone alone, but of a mother's smile, a father's shelter, and the fragrance of belonging.

His father was alive, yet within him too a silence reigned. When Chandrabhushan sat down to study, he would feel his father's eyes resting on him, with a mix of hope, worry, and loneliness.

He understood now that a home runs on two things: a mother's love and a father's restraint. With one gone and the other shattered, the entire house seemed suspended in mid-air.

On the day of the examination, his father said only this: "Son, you are now the light of this house. Do not lose heart."

In those words spoke his mother's blessing, his father's support, and the final hope of holding together a broken home.

Chandrabhushan realised that if one relationship in a house falls apart, the walls may still stand but the family collapses. Yet if even one relationship grows strong, light can return even to a fallen home.

Chandrabhushan sat for his tenth-board examinations. Though silence had spread through his house in those days, a strange resolve had awakened within him. The emptiness that kept melting in his heart after his mother's passing refused to bow before his dreams. His father stood silently behind him like a shadow, not speaking, yet offering support every moment.

Every examination paper seemed to test his courage anew. But Chandrabhushan never looked back on any day. He knew that this was no time to live by crying, by stopping, by breaking. It was time to rise, to gather himself, to move forward.

And when the results came, the whole village was astonished: Chandrabhushan had scored 95 percent.

In that moment, the gleam in his father's eyes could not be put into words. It was not pride, it was a blessing, such a blessing as a father gives when he gently pats his son's back and says, "You can do it, son. And you have done it."

For the first time, Chandrabhushan felt within him the realisation: "Though life may wound us, education always makes a way."

After tenth, he stood at the gateway to higher secondary school, as if on the threshold of a new world. New books, new dreams, new goals, all sparkled in his eyes.

But amidst all this, a deep truth dawned on him day by day: Mahamaya, the Great Illusion, is immensely powerful.

No matter how deep the pain a person passes through, no matter how incomplete they feel without a loved one, still the wheel of life does not stop.

The leela of Mahamaya, the Primordial Shakti, is so mighty that even while weeping, a person learns to smile again; even while breaking, learns to mend; and even while scattering, learns to move forward.

This is Mahamaya. Even after the densest darkness of night, she sends light from some direction or another.

Chandrabhushan too, under the shelter of that same Mahamaya, carrying his pain within, with head held high, set out toward higher secondary school.

7: Path of Dreams

After passing the tenth standard, Chandrabhushan had learned not to pause for even a moment. The grief of Savitri Devi's death was lodged in his chest like a silently smouldering fire, yet that same pain made him all the more stubborn. He knew that now he had no option to lose. The fields and farms of the village, the bitterness of the division, his brother's taunts, the family's poverty, all were thorns in his path, but Chandrabhushan went to school with his bag every morning and studied under the lantern every night. His routine was like a pledge of iron: wake at four in the morning, tend to the cows and buffaloes, then walk three kilometres to school; return in the evening to work in the fields, then study through the night. His palms were covered in blisters, yet his eyes held the same passion that his mother had given him.

Meanwhile, Shambhunath and Sunaina's attitude grew ever harsher. Now that Savitri Devi was gone,

Sunaina's anger became even more unbridled. "What will all this studying get him? He buries his head in books day and night. If he worked in the fields, at least there would be some income," she would often say. Shambhunath too began to voice his opinion openly: "Bhabhi is right. We didn't study much either, and we're managing the house." But Chandrabhushan would only say one thing each time: "By my mother's oath, I will change this family's fortune." That sentence was like a mantra for him, steadying him in every adversity.

The twelfth-standard exams were approaching. Chandrabhushan poured all his energy into his studies. He knew this examination would decide the direction of his future. At night, when the whole village was asleep, he would study by the dim light of the lantern. Sometimes hunger came, and he would toast whatever bread was left from the hearth and eat it. Seeing his dedication, some of the village teachers helped him. The master occasionally called him to his home to teach, giving him old books. This was the time when Chandrabhushan realised that education is not merely bookish knowledge, but a weapon that makes a person strong in every battle.

Finally, the day came when Chandrabhushan passed his twelfth in the first division. The whole village talked about his marks. But amidst this joy there was also bitterness, the question of college fees. Shambhunath made it clear that he could not give money for further studies. Yet Chandrabhushan did not lose heart. He decided to go to the city. He knew this path would not be easy, but now he had no choice. Ramlakhan Thakur helped as much as he could and, blessing his son to succeed, saw him off.

In the city, Chandrabhushan began living in a small room. He went to college in the morning and gave tuitions in the evening. Despite this, he remained fully devoted to his studies. Sometimes at night, exhausted, he would fall asleep among his books, but in the morning he would rise with the same zeal. He completed his graduation, continuing his education through hard work and scholarships. Village folk would say, "A boy from a poor family, how far can he really go?" But Chandrabhushan shut these voices out of his mind. He knew that society always looks with suspicion, but success silences such doubts.

Now a new goal stood before Chandrabhushan: preparation for the BPSC (Bihar Public Service Commission). For two years he prepared alone, with only the walls of his room and old textbooks for company. His room became filled with books; important facts and formulas were written on the walls. The memory of Savitri Devi would stir him each time: "My son will become an officer." That sentence was an endless source of inspiration for him. Sometimes fatigue would overcome him, and he would look at his mother's photograph, then plunge back into his studies.

If a person cannot be inspired by the circumstances of his own home, the struggles of his own family, and the harsh truths of his own life, then no teaching in the world, no speech, no great personality can inspire him. Inspiration does not descend from outside, it is born from the fire within. And in a heart that lacks that fire, even mountains remain only piles of stone.

And then came that historic day when Chandrabhushan was selected in the BPSC. The post: Block Development Officer. When he received the news, he sat in silence for several minutes. A stream of tears flowed from his eyes. This was the moment he had imagined for years. Holding the appointment letter, he first looked up at the sky and whispered, "Mother, I have succeeded." He felt as if his mother's smile was showering down upon him from the heavens.

See the irony: the village where once people had underestimated him was now where he was posted. Now those same people, those same brothers, those same relatives looked at him with respect. Shambhunath said with pride, "Now it feels that our youngest has truly increased the family's honour." Sunaina, who once spoke with such bitterness, was silent today. In her eyes was a strange mixture of embarrassment and joy. The village elders remarked, "Despite poverty, division, and taunts, the boy has become an officer. Wealth and position truly change people's eyes."

Hearing all this, Ramlakhan Thakur walked around with his chest puffed out in pride.

But Chandrabhushan smiled and said, "Respect comes not from wealth but from hard work. Hard work is a weapon that can win any battle." And that day, for the first time, it seemed as if Savitri Devi had come alive again, stroking his head. Chandrabhushan felt that his success was not his alone, but belonged to every young person who dares to dream despite hardships. He knew that his real responsibility was beginning now: the development of his village and his society. And to fulfil that responsibility, he was fully prepared with the knowledge that had been his earning over all these years.

In his mind, remembering Mother Bhawani, Chandrabhushan said to himself:

"Life has taught me one thing very deeply. A large part of the world runs not on principles but on circumstances, and the greatest craftsman of circumstances is 'wealth'. Without money, even a person's abilities are imprisoned like a pigeon in a dark room; but with money, those same abilities dance like a peacock. Wealth is the force that breathes respect into relationships, and in its absence, those same relationships become a burden of obligations. This is the bitter truth: it is through wealth that we obtain various 'attainments', brotherhood, belonging, and sometimes even those parents who teach the lesson of equality, yet in practice end up making distinctions among their children.

It is said that parents are impartial, but life is full of exceptions. In a family, if there are two sons, one remains immersed in struggles and the other becomes an officer, then not only society but even the walls of the house begin to feel the difference. For one who has success, doors begin to open by themselves. For the one who does not, he grows weary knocking on those same doors. Love remains, but its form changes, it becomes pride for one son, and a weight of worry for the other.

And then the mind understands that life's first motivator is not external applause, but the family's condition, the struggle, the deprivation amidst which one has grown up. If a person cannot be motivated by his own household circumstances, then no guru in the world, no book, no knowledge can give him direction. A person's true awakening comes through pain, and his true flight begins the moment he understands that circumstances are not to be cursed, but to be turned into stepping stones."

And so, he prepared himself to walk this new path of service.

8: An Unfamiliar Attachment

Evening had fallen, and the last rays of the sun had already taken their leave from the sky. Chandrabhushan was returning from the BDO office, his mind reviewing the day's work. A light November chill was in the air, and a silence had spread through the village's deserted lanes. But today there was something unsettling in the wind, as if something untoward was about to happen. As he reached a bend in the road, he heard voices of some boys, not ordinary conversation. The voices carried a strange tone of teasing and bullying.

"Hey, stop, won't you? We just want to be friends," one boy's voice said.

"Yeah, yeah, we'll drop you home. Why are you scared?" said another.

"What's with all this arrogance? We're from your own village," a third voice declared, its arrogance unmistakable.

Chandrabhushan slowed his bike and looked carefully. A girl of about sixteen or seventeen was walking hurriedly, fear clear on her face. Behind her were five or six boys from the village, and leading them was his own nephew, Lav, the boy he had watched grow up from childhood. Right before his eyes, Lav was walking down the wrong path. For a moment Chandrabhushan's heart stopped. He thought, This is Lav. The same Lav I used to carry on my shoulders. Now he's fallen in with the wrong crowd again. If I let this continue, one day he'll ruin someone's life.

Without wasting a moment, Chandrabhushan pulled his bike directly in front of the boys, as if a wall had suddenly risen. "Hey! All of you, stop." His voice carried both anger and authority, echoing through the lane.

The boys flinched, as if shaken awake. "Uncle... you?" Lav stammered, his face pale. He knew that with his uncle there, no excuse would work.

Chandrabhushan was furious. Anger flashed in his eyes. "Have you no shame? Blocking the way of someone's daughter, someone's sister? Is this what your parents taught you? Shall I call all your parents here right now? Let's see how brave you really are."

The boys started to flee, like mice scattering at the sight of a cat. "Get out of here! Don't show your faces again! If I catch you next time, it'll be a police matter." Chandrabhushan shouted, and the boys vanished into the darkness.

The girl was still trembling, tears in her eyes, her lips quivering. Chandrabhushan said gently, "Don't be afraid. You're safe now. Where is your home? Which village are you from?"

The girl answered hesitantly, "Sir, my name is Rekha. I live in the Harijan Tola over there. I got late from school today, the teacher held extra classes. I didn't think anything like this would happen on the way." Her voice still shook with fear.

Chandrabhushan took a deep breath and said, "Rekha, from now on, if you ever face any trouble, whether with studies or anyone troubling you, come directly to the BDO office, or call this number. I am

Chandrabhushan, the BDO of this village." He wrote his number on a piece of paper and gave it to her.

For the first time, Rekha lifted her head and looked at him, her eyes filled with surprise and gratitude. "Thank you, sir. If you hadn't come today, I don't know what would have happened. I was so scared." Her voice choked.

Chandrabhushan started the bike and said, "Sit, I'll drop you home. Don't go out alone at night. If you ever get delayed, walk with a friend, or ask someone from home to come fetch you."

Rekha sat on the bike hesitantly. Throughout the ride, one thought kept running through Chandrabhushan's mind: That child I saw playing in my lap, whom I taught to ride a bicycle and to read, he is now walking down the wrong path. Where have those days gone when children would return home after playing in the evening? If I hadn't stopped them today, someone's life could have been ruined tomorrow. Lav's life, and that innocent girl's too.

After dropping Rekha near her home, Chandrabhushan stood there for a while. His eyes held a sense of satisfaction. Today he had protected someone's honour, someone's life. But along with that satisfaction came a worry, about Lav and young men like him, about their future. He decided that from the next day, he would do something for the village's youth, guide them in the right direction. Because he knew that was a true officer's greatest duty: not just to work on papers, but to bring positive change into people's lives.

After that night, things began to change slowly, as if the course of a river had been altered. Whenever Chandrabhushan returned from his office, he would often encounter that same girl on the way, sometimes with her school bag slung over her shoulder, sometimes returning from a friend's house. The dark lanes of the village were still not safe for girls, and Chandrabhushan felt deep inside that helping just once was not enough; safety was not a one-time promise, but a continuous responsibility.

It had now become a responsibility for him, yet one that carried not a burden but an easy affection. Every day at that same bend, under that same peepal tree, he would slow his bike and say softly, "Come, I'll drop you. It's already night." At first Rekha would hesitate, "No, sir, I can manage," but seeing the concern in Chandrabhushan's eyes, she could not refuse. Gradually, hesitation turned into habit. Now Rekha said nothing, simply sat behind him with a faint smile, as if it were part of an unspoken understanding. Then Chandrabhushan would drop her near her home, make sure she had gone inside safely, and only then leave. This became a nightly routine, without any promises or formalities, yet as if both hearts had silently agreed that it was necessary.

A few weeks later, a development programme was organised at the village school, a seminar on "Education and Empowerment". Chandrabhushan was invited as chief guest to deliver a speech. He arrived at the stage, dressed in a white kurta-pyjama, and as he glanced over the audience, his eyes once again found her first: Rekha. Today she was being honoured as the school topper, and the prize was to be given by his own hands. On her face was a proud smile, a smile that told the story of a girl who had struggled and succeeded.

When Chandrabhushan called her name into the microphone, "Rekha Kumari, Class Twelve, First Rank" the same trust gleamed in Rekha's eyes that had first appeared that night when he had said, "Don't be afraid, beta. You are safe." She came to the stage, and as she received the award, their eyes met for a moment. It was a pause that needed no words, a pause filled with gratitude, with deep trust, and somewhere, a bond that until now had remained unspoken. Chandrabhushan handed her the prize and said, "Very well done, Rekha. Your hard work has paid off." Rekha smiled and bowed her head.

A few days later, Rekha came to Chandrabhushan's office regarding work under a government scheme, "Nal Jal Yojana" (Tap Water Scheme). A file was in her hand, and her face carried a seriousness that suggested she had come with a real problem. Seeing her at the door, Chandrabhushan was momentarily surprised. He had never imagined Rekha would come to his office.

"Oh, it's you? Come, sit down. What's the matter?" Chandrabhushan gestured toward a chair.

Rekha placed the file on his desk and said, "Sir, our house doesn't get tap water. I thought I'd take your advice on how to avail this scheme."

Chandrabhushan smiled. "Don't call me 'sir', just call me by name. And don't worry, I'll come to your house myself and get it arranged. Just tell me, will tomorrow morning be fine?"

Rekha nodded and went home.

This meeting was different from the earlier ones. There was no dark lane, no silence of night. In the sunlight filtering through the window, Rekha seemed different, confident, eager to solve problems. And Chandrabhushan could not stop the slight quickening of his heartbeat. A heartbeat that was no longer just about concern, but about a new, unfamiliar attachment.

Meanwhile, somewhere in Rekha's heart too, an unspoken sense of belonging had begun to grow, a trust she had never felt with anyone else. Chandrabhushan was not just an officer; he was safety, he was trust, and slowly, he was becoming someone without whom her world felt incomplete.

Chandrabhushan found a good opportunity: he thought of offering her a job as a support worker in his office, and Rekha's parents gave their consent.

Now meetings increased, sometimes on the road, sometimes under the pretext of some file at the office. Each meeting added another thread to the weave of their unspoken relationship. And that unspoken ritual of dropping her home at night had now become a permanent part of both their daily routines, a part without which the day no longer felt complete.

9: Declaration of Love

At night, the village lanes were as deserted as always; only the distant barking of dogs and the rustle of trees broke the silence. Chandrabhushan had gone out to drop Rekha at the road bend, as he did every day. A gentle breeze was blowing, and from somewhere far away came the sweet scent of ripening paddy from the fields, infusing this cold November night with a strange warmth. Rekha was quieter than usual tonight. Something unspoken lingered in her eyes, the moment before a decision, when heart and mind are in dialogue.

Chandrabhushan started the bike. Rekha sat behind him. At first she held the rear handle as she always did, but today something was different. After a while, as the bike passed along the edge of a field, Rekha's fingers came to rest on Chandrabhushan's waist. For the first time today she had held him this way, a touch that was not merely for balance, but an expression of unspoken attraction.

Chandrabhushan's heart beat faster. His breath caught for a moment. This gesture was clear: Rekha's heart too was moving in the same direction where his own mind had wandered for many nights. He knew how much meaning was hidden in that small touch. It was not just a girl steadying herself on a bike; it was a woman reaching out to a man.

After riding some distance, he stopped the bike. Before them stood an old peepal tree, its dense shade filtering the moonlight. "Are you all right?" Chandrabhushan asked with a faint smile, as if merely asking why he had stopped, though both knew the stopping had another reason. Rekha simply lowered her head and smiled. "Hmm." Her silent assent said everything to Chandrabhushan.

Nearby was a small cart where an old man sold kulfi. They stopped there and had some. Chandrabhushan looked at Rekha again and again. In her eyes today there was a different sparkle, the sparkle that comes when one falls in love for the first time. Before the kulfi could melt, Chandrabhushan spoke softly, "Rekha, I want to say something. But I don't know how..." His voice held a strange nervousness, the kind that comes before a first confession of love.

Rekha looked at him with a gentle smile, as if she already knew what was about to happen. There was no surprise in her eyes, only a calm acceptance.

Chandrabhushan's voice grew even softer, as if he were speaking to himself. "Rekha, I've wanted to tell you for a long time. I really like you." The words were so ordinary, yet they held so much: years of loneliness, the emptiness after his mother's passing, and now the new hope that had awakened with this girl.

Rekha's hand gently touched Chandrabhushan's hand. Her touch was a music he had never heard before. This joining of hands was not merely the meeting of two hands, but the meeting of two souls that had grown weary walking separate paths. "I like you too," she said. That was enough.

The nearby fields were quiet, and the starlight spread a silver blanket over the earth. Chandrabhushan looked at Rekha and said softly, "Come, let's sit over there." He pointed to an old cot lying at the edge of the field. They sat down. For a few moments they were silent, then Chandrabhushan gently placed his hand on her shoulder. Rekha did not resist; instead she moved closer to him.

Chandrabhushan turned her face toward him. In the moonlight, Rekha's face seemed even more beautiful. Rekha slipped her arms around Chandrabhushan's neck and drew him closer.

Slowly, the embrace deepened. The stars in the sky twinkled, bearing witness to this love.

They lost themselves in each other so completely that they did not notice where the night disappeared. They lay quietly for a while, Chandrabhushan holding Rekha in his arms. Rekha rested her head on his chest and listened to his heartbeat. "Your heart is beating so fast," she whispered. "Yes, for you," Chandrabhushan said, and stroked her hair.

How long it was before the bike started again, no one could say. Rekha no longer held the rear handle. Her arms were wrapped tightly around Chandrabhushan's waist. On the way, Rekha said, "We'll be a bit late today. My family will ask."

Chandrabhushan said, "I'll drop you. Don't worry."

When she reached home, it was indeed quite late. The door opened and her father asked, "Why are you so late?"

Rekha quickly made an excuse: "A tree had fallen on the road, there was a jam; I had to come by another way." There was a strange tremor in her voice, but she composed herself.

Her family accepted the explanation, and Rekha went into her room.

That night, both went to bed, but neither could sleep. Chandrabhushan lay gazing at the stars through his window, Rekha's memory floating in his mind. Rekha tossed and turned in her bed, every time remembering Chandrabhushan's touch. In their hearts, the first love had kindled like a small flame. This night became the most memorable night of their lives, the night when two lonely hearts met and became one.

10: Duty Path

A new whispering had begun to take birth in the village lanes, like weeds suddenly sprouting in a dry field. People were troubled. Chandrabhushan dropping Rekha home on his motorcycle. The elders sitting at the village square would stroke their beards and say, "As soon as he became an officer, his colours changed. He was fine before, but now alongside his job, he's also taken up dropping off girls." Women at the well would whisper while filling their pitchers, "A boy and a girl spending so much time together isn't right. Besides, she's from the Harijan Tola, and he's from a Thakur family. I don't understand what these people are thinking."

Rekha went to work, but often she was seen returning with Chandrabhushan. This began to prick the neighbours like a thorn. Some burned with jealousy that a Harijan girl was getting a ride from the BDO himself; others found it immoral. Envy, spite, and narrow-mindedness began to pour poison, and this poison slowly spread through the entire village.

One day Rekha's mother called her into the kitchen and asked in a stern voice, "Who is that boy who drops you every day? Do you know what people are saying?" Rekha remained silent, lowering her eyes. Her heart beat fast. She knew that if the truth came out, the fire of society would burn her first. Her honour, her future, everything would turn to ash. She said only, "Mother, he is the BDO sir. He drops me home safely. That's all." But the suspicion in her mother's eyes did not lessen.

Chandrabhushan too sensed all this. He knew how sharp the tongues of the village could be, how an ordinary matter could be blown out of proportion. But his conscience was clear. "If dropping someone safely home is a crime, then I will commit that crime every day. I only helped a person, yet in people's eyes it has become an offence." Still, he went every day to drop Rekha, because for him, Rekha's safety mattered more than the gossip of society.

Their relationship was growing stronger in secret. Each meeting added a new layer of trust, each conversation nurtured a new intimacy. But outside, the walls of society were rising higher, walls built of caste, honour, and old rigidities. Now the story was no longer just about love; it was a confrontation. Heart versus society, love versus tradition, truth versus falsehood. And this confrontation was slowly turning into a fire, a fire that might consume everything.

A few days later.

The gentle morning sun filtered into Rekha's room, but her mind was heavy. For the past few days, she had been feeling strange: dizziness, nausea, and she had lost track of certain dates. At first she thought it was just the changing season or work fatigue, but when the symptoms persisted for a week, a fear settled in her heart. Quietly she went to the village midwife and got checked. What she had suspected turned out to be true: she was pregnant.

In that moment, Rekha's world seemed to stop. Darkness spread before her eyes. She knew what this meant. An unmarried girl pregnant, and that too from a boy of a higher caste. Society would not let her live. That night she met Chandrabhushan, and with tears in her eyes, she told him everything.

At first Chandrabhushan could not believe it. Then, as the reality sank in, a strange calm came over him. He knew that now only two paths lay before them: either he abandoned Rekha, which was impossible for him, or he married her. He embraced Rekha and said, "Don't be afraid. I am here. We will marry."

But Chandrabhushan knew it would not be so easy. He decided to speak first with his father, Ramlakhan. One evening when he went home, he sat before his father and said, "Pita ji, I want to marry a girl."

Ramlakhan asked, "Who is the girl? Which village is she from? What is her caste?"

Chandrabhushan told the truth: "She is from this village. Rekha Kumari. She lives in the Harijan Tola."

Hearing this, Ramlakhan's face turned red. "What? A Harijan girl? Have you lost your mind? We are a Thakur family. A Harijan daughter-in-law in our house? Never! This would be a betrayal of our caste, of our ancestors!"

Chandrabhushan tried to reason: "Father, caste is just a word. Rekha is a good girl. Educated."

But Ramlakhan cut him off: "No! Absolutely not! I will never allow this marriage. You may leave your job, leave this house, but this marriage will not happen."

Chandrabhushan did not tell him that Rekha was pregnant. He knew that if that came out, the situation would become even worse. He silently rose and left, but his mind was made up. He would marry Rekha, no matter what.

Over the next few days, Chandrabhushan made a plan. He told Rekha, "We must elope and marry. Here, this marriage is impossible." Rekha agreed. She was afraid, but she trusted Chandrabhushan.

One night, while the whole village slept, Chandrabhushan and Rekha left. Chandrabhushan took Rekha on his bike, and they set off toward the city. Throughout the ride, Rekha's heart pounded, swinging between fear and hope. Chandrabhushan held her hand and said, "Don't be afraid. I am with you."

In the city, they went to a temple and performed a Gandharva marriage. No feast, no elaborate rituals, just the union of two hearts. Chandrabhushan put a mangalsutra around Rekha's neck and placed vermilion on her forehead. At that moment, tears filled both their eyes, tears of joy, tears of struggle, tears of hope for a new beginning.

When they returned to the village after the marriage, a storm erupted. Ramlakhan threw Chandrabhushan out of the house. The villagers declared a social boycott against them. Rekha's family too faced the taunts of society. But Chandrabhushan and Rekha did not give up. They rented a small room outside the village and began their new life.

It was not easy. Chandrabhushan's job came under threat because some influential people in the village began filing complaints against him. But they held each other's hands. Chandrabhushan said, "We have decided to stay together, so we will face every difficulty together."

And so began Chandrabhushan and Rekha's new battle, a battle that was not only a test of their love but also a challenge to the thinking of the entire society.

11: Birth and Bond

That night's silence was filled with a strange pain, as if the air itself were sobbing. Even the stars in the sky seemed to have closed their eyes, afraid that they might witness something they shouldn't. In the small rented room where Chandrabhushan and Rekha had begun to build their world, a new sun was about to rise. Rekha's cries echoed off the walls, and Chandrabhushan's heart beat in rhythm with those sounds, half fear, half hope.

When the first light of dawn pierced the darkness, a little son had already been born into Rekha's arms. His tiny eyes were closed, his fists clenched, as if unaware of the storms of this world. When Chandrabhushan saw his son for the first time, tears flowed from his eyes, tears that held joy, fear, and the weight of a heavy responsibility. Rekha was also crying; in her tears was the pain that every mother feels when she knows her child has come into a world that does not accept him.

"What shall we name him?" Rekha asked in a tired voice.

Chandrabhushan lovingly touched the child's forehead. "Chandresh. We will name him Chandresh, 'lord of the moon'." But it was not just a name. Chandrabhushan knew that this child was not merely a baby. He was a question, a challenge to a society still shackled by caste. This child would ask: Is there any caste greater than love? Is there any tradition above humanity?

But the soil of the village was soaked in centuries of poison. As soon as news of Chandresh's birth spread, a fire erupted. It was a fire of hatred, of a way of thinking that was afraid to break. Rekha's family felt as if their honour had been trampled in the dust. Prestige, caste, false pride, everything flared up together.

Rekha's father, who had remained silent until then, now spoke out: "Bring our daughter back. This child will not grow up in our house." When Chandrabhushan and Rekha refused, he filed a police report. The story was twisted on paper: "abduction", "seduction", "eloping with a minor". Truth was bent into falsehood. Yes, Rekha had been seventeen at the time of marriage, and in the eyes of the law she was a minor. That fact was turned into a weapon.

One morning, as Chandrabhushan sat holding Chandresh in his arms, the police arrived. Rekha was forcibly taken away with her parents. Chandresh was snatched from Chandrabhushan's hands and given to Rekha's mother. Rekha's screams struck the walls and returned: "My child! Give me back my child!" But no one listened.

And Chandrabhushan, who had just become a father, who had only learned to love, who had never harmed anyone, his wrists were bound in handcuffs. His eyes were fixed on Chandresh, who was now crying. He said, "Take care of my son." But his voice was lost in the clank of the handcuffs.

When the prison gate closed, it was not merely a man who was imprisoned. A dream was imprisoned, the dream of love, of equality. A family was imprisoned, Chandrabhushan, Rekha, and Chandresh's family. And an era was imprisoned, that era when people believed love could change everything. Through the lock went trust, went love, went the dream that Chandrabhushan had inherited from his mother.

Sitting in the darkness of the jail cell, Chandrabhushan's eyes still held a light. That light was not of despair, but of hope. That light was the memory of his son, Chandresh. Chandresh's innocent face, his tiny fingers, his first smile, these memories became a lamp for Chandrabhushan. He knew that now his battle was not only for his love, but for his son's future. What kind of society would Chandresh grow up to see? Would he feel shame at his parent's love, or pride?

In that cell, Chandrabhushan made a promise: he would come out, and he would not only reunite his family, but also change the society that had brought him here. That promise became his strength, his support. And that light, that promise, would become the rest of the story, a story not only of one family, but of the transformation of an entire society. Chandrabhushan knew that countless Chandreshes would be born into this society, and it was his responsibility to build a better world for all of them.

The night was heavy, as if a stone had been placed on the chest. Rekha had been locked in a small dark room in her own family's house, a padlock hanging on the door. In the outer room, her newborn son was crying, and with every wail Rekha's heart broke. Her mother held the child tightly in her lap, but even though she could, she would not take him to Rekha. Family fear, societal pressure, and caste pride were stronger than that child's cries.

A storm raged inside Rekha. Waves of fear drowned her, the fire of helplessness burned her, and the screams of maternal love were stuck in her throat. She knew her child was just beyond a wall, but reaching him felt like crossing an ocean. Her mobile phone had been taken; they were trying to silence her. But her younger sister, Suruchi, whose eyes still held innocence, slipped an old phone through the crack in the door. It was their mother's phone, which Suruchi had secretly picked up.

Rekha's hand trembled. Her fingers shook so much that dialling a number was difficult. Whom should she call? The police? The police had already turned against her. Then she remembered, Chandrabhushan's father, Ramlakhan Thakur. Would he listen? Would he help? She had no other option now.

With shaking hands, she dialled Ramlakhan Thakur's number. One ring, two, three, then a voice came: "Hello, who is this?" Ramlakhan Thakur's voice carried fatigue, worry.

As soon as the call connected, Rekha could only manage to say, "Pita ji, save my child. My family has imprisoned us." Then her voice choked. Tears drowned her words. But in that broken voice was so much that it melted the listener's heart.

On the other end, Ramlakhan Thakur's eyes filled with tears. As soon as he heard the voice, he recognised Rekha. The pain in her voice was not just the pain of a woman; it was the pain of a mother. He recalled the child's face in his mind, that innocent face he had seen a few days ago. His heart filled with compassion. Years of rigid traditions, caste pride, fear of society, all of it broke in that one moment. He immediately called his eldest son, Shambhunath.

Worry was written on Shambhunath's face. "What happened, Pita ji?"

Ramlakhan Thakur took a deep breath and said, "Son, Rekha called. Her child has been taken away from her." Then, after a pause, he said, "Listen, Shambhu. When Chandrabhushan held her hand, she became our daughter-in-law. Now it is our duty to protect her. Whatever society may say, we cannot abandon our daughter-in-law and our grandson."

Shambhunath saw a new resolve in his father's eyes. He knew this decision would not be easy. But he nodded. "As you say, Pita ji."

Within hours, Shambhunath, along with some respected men of the village, the former sarpanch, the school headmaster, and a few others, reached Rekha's parent's house. The name and standing of the Thakur family carried weight; Rekha's family could say nothing against them. Shambhunath stated clearly,

"Rekha is now our family's daughter-in-law, and this child is our grandson. We are taking them with us."

There was some argument, some objections, but under the pressure of the Thakur family and the presence of the village elders, Rekha's family had to relent. They brought Rekha and her child away.

When Rekha arrived at the Thakur doorstep, she touched Ramlakhan Thakur's feet with trembling hands. Tears streamed from her eyes, these were not tears of fear, but of relief, of gratitude. Ramlakhan Thakur lifted her and said, "Daughter, this is your home now. Do not be afraid."

She was taken inside the house. The same courtyard where her in-laws had once refused to accept her was now open for her. Sunaina, who had always been considered harsh and had always opposed Chandrabhushan and Rekha's relationship, stepped forward silently. She placed her hand on Rekha's forehead, like a mother and said, "This house is yours now. Do not be afraid. Your child is our child."

Hearing this, Rekha's eyes again filled with tears, but now these tears were not of pain. They were tears of relief, of trust. Half her crisis had been lifted. Now she had a home, a family that accepted her. But the story was not over. Chandrabhushan was still in prison. Their love was still a question before the law and society. But today Rekha had found a new hope, hope that she was no longer alone, hope that this battle of love she was not fighting alone. And with that hope, she was ready to move forward.

12: Victory of Faith

When the first light of dawn descended upon the courtyard, it was not merely the sun's rays but the first beam of a new hope. Rekha's eyes, though she had remained awake all night, held not the weariness of sleeplessness but a deep faith. Her mind was lost in the sound of the temple bells, those same morning bells that had been ringing in this house for years. She slowly sat down before the small temple in the corner of the house, the same temple where Savitri Devi once lit lamps and prayed for Chandrabhushan's future. Today, this temple was Rekha's last hope.

With trembling hands folded, eyes closed, she spoke to Mother Bhawani: "O Mother, now everything is in your hands. My mangalya, my child, all are at your feet. I have committed no sin; I only loved. If this is a sin, then I accept this sin. But Mother, my child is innocent, my husband is innocent. Save them, Mother."

The tears that dropped from her eyes, meeting the flame of the lamp, became a silent poem. In every tear was a history, a history of fear, of struggle, and of love. And amidst these tears, her heart began to hum: "When the world loses, faith wins; when bonds break, a mother's lap mends." This was not mere humming; it was a prayer, a whisper of last hope.

Within the high walls of the prison, sitting in a small cell, Chandrabhushan was thinking only of one thing: "I have committed no sin; I only loved. That love which my mother taught me, that love which makes a human being human." Before his eyes floated Rekha's face and Chandresh's smile. He knew that today in court his future would be decided, but he trusted in his innocence. He trusted in the love he and Rekha had built together.

The next day, the courtroom was crowded. Lawyers from the village and the city, curious eyes, everything hinged on that one case that would decide not only the future of two people but also hold a mirror to society's thinking. When Rekha was called to the witness box, she wore a red saree, and on her face was a remarkable calm. Without trembling, without fear, in clear and firm words she said, "All of this happened of my own will. No one abducted or seduced me. I love Chandrabhushan, and he is my husband. Our marriage took place in a temple, before God."

Her voice carried such truth that it struck the walls and reached every heart. The judge solemnly turned through the file, examined the record of age, read Rekha's statement, and then said quietly, "The law cannot break a happy family. This marriage is valid. The complaint is dismissed. Chandrabhushan is to be released immediately."

A silence fell over the courtroom and then that silence broke, transforming into a wave of relief. Tears flowed from Chandrabhushan's eyes, but these tears were not of bondage; they were of liberation.

Outside the door, the little child Chandresh, playing in Sunaina's lap, stretched his arms toward his mother. As soon as Chandrabhushan ran out, he lifted his son into his arms and held him tightly to his chest. Rekha stepped forward and grasped his trembling hands. This reunion of the three was no ordinary reunion. It was the mending of shattered dreams, the reuniting of a scattered family.

Ramlakhan Thakur's eyes were moist. He said in a quiet voice, "Now this family will not break; now it will be complete." In his words were years of pain, years of struggle, and now years of peace.

And in that moment, the three, Chandrabhushan, Rekha, and Chandresh, looked at one another as if years of separation, years of pain, years of struggle had dissolved in that single moment. Chandrabhushan embraced Rekha and said, "Now we will never be parted." And Rekha answered only with a smile, because now there was no need for words.

Now the village too was changing. The same village that had once opposed their love was slowly accepting it. People were beginning to understand that in love there is no caste, no high or low. And the real struggle of the story was about to begin, a new struggle, a struggle of new responsibilities, the struggle to build a new society.

That day, in the courtyard of the court, when the scales of justice tipped toward truth, not merely a case was settled. A life that was breaking was mended; a family that was scattering was restored. Chandrabhushan, Rekha, and little Chandresh, holding one another's hands, walked out of the courthouse. Outside, the sun was shining, and in its light their future shone as well.

Amidst the temple bells, Rekha silently bowed to Mother Bhawani. Chandrabhushan remembered his struggle and felt that his parent's efforts, tears, and blessings had not gone in vain. The soil of the village, which had once struck him with hardship, had today given him recognition and respect.

Now there was no fear in their lives, only faith. No struggle, only discipline. No humiliation, only honour. And with this faith, Chandrabhushan returned to his small world, where now there was not only pain but love, responsibility, the warmth of family, and the light of the future.

Even after crashing against every wall of society, love remained alive, because where truth was, there was Chandrabhushan.

www.ingramcontent.com/pod-product-compliance
Lightning Source LLC
LaVergne TN
LVHW090426210926
848480LV00002B/697